# BASEBALL LEGENDS

Hank Aaron
Grover Cleveland Alexander
Ernie Banks
Albert Belle
Johnny Bench
Yogi Berra
Barry Bonds
Roy Campanella
Roberto Clemente
Ty Cobb
Dizzy Dean
Joe DiMaggio
Bob Feller
Jimmie Foxx
Lou Gehrig
Bob Gibson
Ken Griffey, Jr.
Rogers Hornsby
Walter Johnson
Sandy Koufax
Greg Maddux
Mickey Mantle
Christy Mathewson
Willie Mays
Stan Musial
Satchel Paige
Mike Piazza
Cal Ripken, Jr.
Brooks Robinson
Frank Robinson
Jackie Robinson
Babe Ruth
Tom Seaver
Duke Snider
Warren Spahn
Willie Stargell
Frank Thomas
Honus Wagner
Ted Williams
Carl Yastrzemski
Cy Young

## CHELSEA HOUSE PUBLISHERS

BASEBALL LEGENDS

# FRANK THOMAS

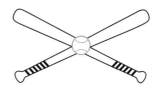

*Carrie Muskat*

*Introduction by*
*Jim Murray*

---

*Senior Consultant*
*Earl Weaver*

CHELSEA HOUSE PUBLISHERS
*Philadelphia*

*Cover photo credit*: AP/Wide World Photo

**Produced by Choptank Syndicate, Inc.**

*Editor and Picture Researcher*: Norman L. Macht
*Production Coordinator and Editorial Assistant*: Mary E. Hull
*Designer*: Lisa Hochstein
*Cover Designer*: Alison Burnside

1 3 5 7 9 8 6 4 2

Library of Congress Cataloging-in-Publication Data

Muskat, Carrie.
      Frank Thomas / Carrie Muskat; introduction by Jim Murray;
senior consultant, Earl Weaver.
         p.  cm. — (Baseball legends)
      Includes bibliographical references and index.
      Summary:  A biography of the Chicago White Sox slugger who
came to be known as "The Big Hurt" for his prowess with the
bat.
      ISBN 0-7910-4381-9
      1. Thomas, Frank, 1968- —Juvenile literature.
2. Baseball players—United States—Biography—Juvenile
literature. 3. Chicago White Sox (Baseball team)—Juvenile
literature. [1. Thomas, Frank, 1968-  . 2. Baseball
players. 3. Afro-Americans—Biography.] I. Weaver, Earl,
1930-  . II. Title. III. Series.
GV865.T45M87  1997
796.357'092—dc21
  [B]                                              97-5505
                                                      CIP
                                                       AC

# CONTENTS

# WHAT MAKES A STAR

*Jim Murray*

No one has ever been able to explain to me the mysterious alchemy that makes one man a .350 hitter and another player, more or less identical in physical makeup, hard put to hit .200. You look at an Al Kaline, who played with the Detroit Tigers from 1953 to 1974. He was pale, stringy, almost poetic-looking. He always seemed to be struggling against a bad case of mononucleosis. But with a bat in his hands, he was King Kong. During his career, he hit 399 home runs, rapped out 3,007 hits, and compiled a .297 batting average.

Form isn't the reason. The first time anybody saw Roberto Clemente step into the batter's box for the Pittsburgh Pirates, the best guess was that Clemente would be back in Double A ball in a week. He had one foot in the bucket and held his bat at an awkward angle—he looked as though he couldn't hit an outside pitch. A lot of other ballplayers may have had a better-looking stance. Yet they never led the National League in hitting in four different years, the way Clemente did.

Not every ballplayer is born with the ability to hit a curveball. Nor is exceptional hand-eye coordination the key to heavy hitting. Big league locker rooms are filled with players who have all the attributes, save one: discipline. Every baseball man can tell you a story about a pitcher who throws a ball faster than anyone has ever seen but who has no control on or *off* the field.

The Hall of Fame is full of people who transformed themselves into great ballplayers by working at the sport, by studying the game, and making sacrifices. They're overachievers—and winners. If you want to find them, just watch the World Series. Or simply read about New York Yankee great Lou Gehrig; Ted Williams, "the Splendid Splinter" of the Boston Red Sox; or the Dodgers' strikeout king Sandy Koufax.

A pitcher *should* be able to win a lot of ballgames with a 98-miles-per-hour fastball. But what about the pitcher who wins 20 games a year with a fastball so slow that you can catch it with your teeth? Bob Feller of the Cleveland Indians got into the Hall of Fame with a blazing fastball that glowed in the dark. National League star Grover Cleveland Alexander got there with a pitch that took considerably longer to reach the plate; but when it did arrive, the pitch was exactly where Alexander wanted it to be—and the last place the batter expected it to be.

There are probably more players with exceptional ability who didn't make it to the major leagues than there are who did. A number of great hitters, bored with fielding practice, had to be dropped from their team because their home-run production didn't make up for their lapses in the field. And then there are players like Brooks Robinson of the Baltimore Orioles, who made himself into a human vacuum cleaner at third base because he knew that working hard to become an expert fielder would win him a job in the big leagues.

A star is not something that flashes through the sky. That's a comet. Or a meteor. A star is something you can steer ships by. It stays in place and gives off a steady glow; it is fixed, permanent. A star works at being a star.

And that's how you tell a star in baseball. He shows up night after night and takes pride in how brightly he shines. He's Willie Mays running so hard his hat keeps falling off; Ty Cobb sliding to stretch a single into a double; Lou Gehrig, after being fooled in his first two at-bats, belting the next pitch off the light tower because he's taken the time to study the pitcher. Stars never take themselves for granted. That's why they're stars.

# 1

# THE BIG HURT

"I just think I should get a hit every time up."
— Frank Thomas

**F**rank Thomas was on a mission. In his rookie year in 1991, the Chicago White Sox first baseman had batted .318 and hit 32 home runs. His impressive debut earned him third place in the Most Valuable Player balloting behind Cal Ripken Jr. and Cecil Fielder. The next year, he hit .323 as the White Sox designated hitter. He played in all but two games that season and tied for the league lead in doubles and walks. But he slipped to eighth in the MVP voting by the Baseball Writers Association of America, which chose closer Dennis Eckersley for the award. "The MVP is not a pitcher's award," an angry Thomas said. Even though he did not play on defense, Thomas felt he deserved more recognition for his hitting. And he certainly should not have lost to a pitcher. Opposing pitchers knew it did not pay to make Frank Thomas mad.

"I've got a lot to prove," Thomas said. "I hope to play 10, 15 years, and I don't just want to play. I want to do things that have never been done before."

One swing of his big bat was so strong, he hurt the ball. Ken Harrelson, a former major league player and a broadcaster for the Chicago White Sox, had been quick to come up with a nickname for Thomas early in his career: "The Big Hurt."

*In just three years, Frank Thomas became the most feared hitter in the American League. Some commentators anticipated that on some occasions pitchers would rather walk him intentionally with the bases loaded than pitch to him, something that had not happened in the league since 1901.*

Frank Thomas was big. His arms and chest and legs were humongous, as if someone stuck a bicycle air pump into his mouth and inflated his body to near bursting proportions. His bulging biceps stretched the sleeves of his jersey. Thomas's 32-ounce bats looked like toothpicks in his big hands.

"I call him 'Bigger Than Average,'" White Sox coach Doug Mansolino said.

There was no doubting Thomas could hit. He was a natural at the plate, but he had struggled playing first base and was a liability on the field for the White Sox, who had finished third in the American League West in 1992. He wanted to be known as a complete player, and that meant playing better defense. It was one thing to launch 400-foot home runs; it was something else to be sure-handed, quick-footed and an accurate thrower. Thomas arrived at spring training camp early in 1993 to drill with Mansolino, a fiery sparkplug who came up to the middle of the first baseman's massive chest. "He was motivated by the fact that he wants to be MVP—and there's nothing wrong with that," Mansolino said. "In order to do that, your club's got to win and you've got to be an all-around type of player."

In 1993, only his third season in the big leagues, Thomas proved he was better than most. He got off to a slow start and did not connect on his first home run until April 26, a three-run, first-inning shot off Baltimore's Fernando Valenzuela. Two days later, he hit a two-run blast against Milwaukee. On April 30, Thomas belted his second career grand slam and drove in five runs in a 10-2 victory over Toronto. He was just warming up.

In June, he put together an 18-game hitting streak as the White Sox moved into first place in the American League West. Just to put things in perspective: he hit his 24th home run on July 25 against the Milwaukee Brewers, the White Sox's 97th game that season. The previous year, he had totaled 24 home runs in 160 games.

His approach was simple: "I just think I should get a hit every time up." Pitchers could find no weaknesses. Thomas was rarely fooled at the plate. Off-speed pitches or fastballs, inside or out, it did not matter to him. He would wait for his pitch. Hitting coach Walt Hriniak did not have to tinker much with Thomas' mechanics but worked at keeping the "Big Hurt" mentally focused. The two would talk hitting, discuss pitchers' tendencies, analyze situations. Thomas had exceptional eyes and was able to see pitches in his hitting zone. Some felt he could call a game better than most umpires. And he was strong. In the tenth inning of a game against New York,

*Thomas had to work hard to improve his shaky defensive play. His size—6-foot-5 and 257 pounds—made it difficult for him to be graceful. But he takes as much pride in a good fielding play as a home run.*

Thomas hit a line drive over the head of Yankees pitcher Steve Farr. "I thought for sure Bernie Williams, the centerfielder, was going to catch it on a line," Hriniak said, "but the ball kept rising. If it hadn't hit the seats, it might still be going."

Thomas earned a lot of respect that year. "Someday soon," Harrelson said, "we will see a team intentionally walk Frank with the bases loaded. And when they do, I will stand up and applaud them for their intelligence. In my 30 years in this game, I have never seen anyone like him. In another 30 years we may be talking about Frank Thomas in the same way we talk about Ted Williams."

During a series against the White Sox, a group of New York players pondered ways to control the Big Hurt. Sitting in the clubhouse at Yankee Stadium, they discussed strategies, but each suggestion was dismissed. Finally, one player said: "We should just walk him every time up. It can't get any worse."

Thomas almost got a hit every at-bat in August, batting .333 with 10 home runs. And they were clutch hits: six of his homers put the White Sox ahead in the game and two more tied the score. "You go up there after his at-bat and the catcher is just stunned," said Chicago third baseman Robin Ventura, who batted cleanup behind Thomas. "He'll say his guy threw a good pitch and Frank smoked it. Catchers act like I should be amazed going up there. At first, it was, 'God, that guy's lucky,' but he hits a pitcher's good pitches hard. It's not surprising to see him do that."

On September 11, Thomas hit his 41st home run of the season, a franchise record. But it would be his last for the year. Six games later at Oakland Coliseum, he crashed into the fence chasing a foul ball and suffered a deep bruise to the back of his left arm. The White Sox held their breath. Although he tried to play with the pain, he was finally forced out of the lineup on September 27—the day the White Sox clinched the divison with a 4–2 victory over the Seattle Mariners.

The injury did nothing to tarnish a spectacular season. In 1993, he became the fifth player in baseball history to hit .300 with 20 or more home runs, 100 RBI, 100 walks, and 100 runs scored in three consecutive seasons, joining an elite crowd. The others were all in the Hall of Fame: Jimmie Foxx (1934-36), Ted Williams (1946-49), Lou Gehrig (1929-32, 1934-37), and Babe Ruth (1919-21, 1926-28). Remember, Frank Thomas was only 25 years old.

Baseball's most elusive honor was the Triple Crown: winning the league's home run, RBI and average honors. Thomas came close, finishing sixth in average (.317), third in homers (41) and second in RBI (128).

But his favorite play that season was not a home run or a double. It was a defensive play Thomas made at first base. "I dove to my right," he said, "then threw home to get the runner. I don't think I could have made that play before this year."

It was a magical season for Thomas. The Baseball Writers Association of America could not ignore him this time in their balloting for Most Valuable Player. Thomas became the eighth player to be unanimously chosen the American League's MVP. All 28 ballots named him the winner.

"It's a great honor," he said at the time, "but I won't be overly satisfied with this award."

# 2

# BORN TO PLAY BALL

"It was sad. It affected me."
— Frank Thomas

Ida Bell Stroy could tell her grandson, Frank, had a gift. He was not that big when he was born in Columbus, Georgia, on May 27, 1968, weighing 7 1/2 pounds. But as soon as young Frank Thomas could walk, Ida saw something, and spent part of her Social Security check buying him a baseball bat and balls. "This boy's going to be something someday," Ida told her daughter, Charlie Mae. "He loves to play ball."

Frank's father, Frank Thomas, Sr., was a bail bondsman and a deacon in the Nazareth Baptist Church in Columbus, while his mother, Charlie Mae, was an inspector at the Cannon textile mill in nearby Phenix City, Alabama. The youngest of three sisters and a brother, young Frank spent many hours at the East Columbus Boys Club, playing games with kids both older and younger. He was not intimidated by the bigger boys in the club, and one day dragged his father to a Pop Warner football game at Edgewood Park. Frank Jr. was nine years old at the time, and many of the boys on the team were 12. "Dad," Frank said, "I can play with any of those boys." Frank Sr. talked to the coach, Chester Murray, who agreed to put young Frank on the field for one play, lining him

*When Thomas was nine years old, he was bowling over bigger would-be tacklers as a tight end in Pop Warner League games. He starred in baseball, football, and basketball at Columbus (Ga) High School.*

15

up at tight end. Murray called a pass play to Thomas, who caught the ball, bowled over would-be tacklers and ran for a touchdown. "You're my starting tight end," the coach said.

Yet Frank Thomas's life was not always touchdowns and home runs. A younger sister, Pamela, who was born when Frank was eight, became his pride and joy. He would carry her on his shoulders throughout the neighborhood, play with her and protect her. But on Labor Day in 1977, tiny two-year-old Pamela could not get out of bed. She was diagnosed with leukemia. Neither family doctors nor specialists at Emory University Hospital in Atlanta could help. There was no cure. She died on Thanksgiving Day.

Years later, Frank Thomas still could not talk easily about his baby sister. "It was sad. It affected me," he said. "But it's something you don't look back on."

Sports became an escape for Thomas. At the age of 10, he played Peach League baseball games at Wilkinson Field, surrounded by pine trees and the Wercoba Creek. Coaches could not believe he was so talented at such a young age and seemed so much wiser than his years. "He was aware of himself, but he was aware of the other kids, too," coach Jack Key said. "He was very sensitive." He was also very skilled, and Bobby Howard, the baseball coach at Columbus High School, saw a potential superstar in Thomas. The first time Howard watched Thomas play was in a Babe Ruth League game. The right-handed hitter had three hits, all to the opposite field.

High school was a turning point for Thomas. Coach Howard believed in discipline. He made his players run and lift weights. Thomas did not really like to do either at first. "I've had a couple coaches give me a stiff kick when I needed it," Thomas recalled, "and Bobby was the first one to really stick it to me." The strength work showed immediate results. Thomas's home runs often crashed through the windows of a three-story school building 300 feet down the left field line from home plate. During batting practice, he would launch some balls onto the building's roof.

Thomas had a selective eye at a young age. During one high school game, an opposing pitcher tried to beat the Columbus Devils by throwing only changeups and curveballs the first two times through the batting order. When Thomas came up to bat the third time, the pitcher fired a fastball for the first time in the game. "Frank deposited it about 420 feet away," Howard said. "Now I was an All-American in college, hit .400, and I told the kids in the dugout, 'No way could I have even swung at that pitch.'"

After his sophomore year, the realities of life hit Thomas in the face like a fastball. He did not need a summer job, but decided some extra money would allow him to buy some of the things he craved, like clothes and music. That summer, Thomas did physical labor at a Columbus mill, working from 7 a.m. until 3 p.m. It was not fun; he would collapse on his bed each night, exhausted from the full day of work. "That job gave me respect for life," Thomas said. "I knew then what a real 9-to-5 job was, and I knew I didn't want my life to be like that. That's when I really made the commitment to myself that I was going to be a pro someday."

Thomas returned for his junior year four inches taller (6 feet 4 inches now) and leaner by 25 pounds. He starred in three sports at Columbus

High—baseball, football and basketball—and was named All-State and Bi-City Player of the Year in baseball his senior season.

Even though he had mentally made the commitment to baseball, some baseball people were not convinced. In June 1986, he waited at home hoping to get a phone call from a major league team, saying they had drafted him. The call never came. Scouts thought Thomas was a football player dabbling in baseball. He had not had time to practice at first base as much as other players available, so he was lacking defensive skills.

"A lot of pro scouts in this area covered their tracks to the point of fabrication," Auburn baseball coach Hal Baird said later of the excuses made by major league teams who ignored Thomas in the draft that year. "They felt he

*Bobby Howard, Thomas's high school baseball coach, recognized Frank's talent the first time he saw him in a Babe Ruth League game. But Howard drove Thomas as hard as the other players with his workouts and discipline. "Bobby was the first one to really stick it to me," Thomas said.*

wasn't good enough—those were the pure and simple reasons he wasn't drafted. He simply wasn't evaluated correctly."

The rejection bothered Thomas. Several players whom he had competed against were headed to minor league camps. He felt he could play the game better than they could. The scouts had underestimated his competitive desire and misunderstood how important baseball was to him.

Auburn University was hoping it could convince Thomas his future was in football. The school offered Thomas a football scholarship with the promise that he could play baseball. He accepted.

# 3

# CONVINCING
# THE SCOUTS

"He could be in the Hall of Fame."
— Auburn coach Hal Baird

**A**uburn baseball coach Hal Baird knew how special Frank Thomas was the instant Thomas stepped up to the plate the first time for Auburn in the spring of 1987 and hit a line drive. "There's our number four hitter for the next three years," said Baird, projecting Thomas' collegiate career would be cut short when he would be eligible again for the major league draft in his junior year.

In his first Southeastern Conference game against Georgia, Thomas showed the patient eye he had for pitches. "They had him 0–2, 1–2 [in the count], and were throwing him borderline pitches," Baird said, "and he's taking them. Taking them." Most batters would be swinging at anything near the strike zone but Thomas, who was then a massive 6-foot-5 and 230 pounds, had the discipline to wait.

"I told Frank from the start, 'Other than George Brett, you have the best approach to hitting I've seen,'" Baird said. "And by his junior year, I thought [Thomas] was better. He was at a level of refinement I've never seen in a college player before. I'd like to say I taught him. But I think it's a gift."

*Thomas went to Auburn University on a football scholarship as a potential All-American tight end, but he preferred baseball. Knee injuries caused him to drop football in his sophomore year.*

In the summer of 1987, Thomas was named to the U.S. Pan American baseball team. He was the youngest member of the team at the age of 19, but once again, Thomas did not feel intimidated by the older kids and batted .338. He thought he had a spot locked up, but ran out of time. Thomas felt obligated to the Auburn football team, which had given him the scholarship. A man of his word, Thomas left the Pan-Am baseball team before the games even started and reported for football practice on August 20.

It was the right decision but ended the wrong way. In the football team's first full-contact drill, Thomas was hit from behind and suffered strained ligaments in his knee. He still dressed for the first three games of the football season, but reinjured his knee in the third game against Tennessee. He then approached Auburn football coach Pat Dye. It was time to concentrate on baseball. "I could see this coming, Frank, but I'd like you to reconsider," said Dye, who thought Thomas had the potential to be an All-American tight end. Frank had not seen much action, catching three passes for 45 yards, but Dye knew the special talent Thomas possessed.

Dye asked Auburn baseball coach Hal Baird about Thomas's future on the diamond. "Coach," Baird said, "he could be in the Hall of Fame."

In his first season on the Auburn baseball team, Thomas batted .359 and hit 21 home runs. In 1988, his sophomore year, opposing teams decided that rather than let him beat them, they would not pitch to him. Thomas responded by expanding his strike zone and batted .385. His home runs were mammoth shots. At Mississippi State, he cleared the 325-foot sign on the left field fence as well as the trucks and fans and tailgaters gathered behind the wall. In his junior season, Thomas hit .403 with 19 homers and 19 doubles. His slugging percentage was an unbelievable .801.

Major league scouts paid attention. The White Sox first heard about Thomas after a game in his freshman year against Tennessee. Scout Tom Calvano was stunned at this large, powerful first baseman and called Al Goldis, director of scouting and player development for the White Sox, with the news. "I saw a King Kong hitter today," Calvano said. Thomas dazzled everyone in a home run hitting contest in the Cape Cod League in 1988, outslugging Mo Vaughn, Tim Salmon and Jeff Bagwell. Thomas hit pitch after pitch after pitch over the fences, each one a towering smash that defied gravity.

Mike Rizzo, then a scout for the White Sox, started following Thomas in his junior year. He could tell almost immediately that this was a special player. It was not just the powerful swing but Thomas's approach to the game that impressed Rizzo. "When he went between the lines, he was all business," Rizzo said. "He had a game plan every time he went up to the plate. Rarely did you see him go out of the strike zone. Even in batting practice, he wasn't one of those guys who would put on a massive show of power." Most powerful right-handed hitters pull the ball to left field but Thomas could skillfully hit the ball to all fields.

Whenever he hit the ball, he hit it hard. And whenever he walked onto the field for batting practice, a hush fell over the ballpark. Hot dog vendors would pause, other players would stop their warmups, people would turn their heads. Everyone wanted to watch Frank Thomas hit.

*Thomas blasted towering home runs for Auburn. One White Sox scout said, "I saw a King Kong hitter today." But Thomas was not highly regarded by most scouts; the Major League scouting bureau ranked him 81st among all prospects.*

Each game he scouted, Rizzo became more convinced that Thomas could be an impact first baseman for a major league team. In his original report, Rizzo wrote that Thomas would be one of the top offensive producers in the game. "He could situation hit, he could mash with anybody," Rizzo said. "He could hit it as far as anybody. But what separated him from other big masher type of hitters was that he'll hit for average."

Many scouts still thought they were seeing a football player wearing a baseball uniform. Rizzo was not worried. As big as he was, Thomas also possessed quick feet and soft hands, necessities to be a good first baseman. He ran the bases well and had good speed. "His awesome size didn't bother me—I thought it was an asset," Rizzo said. "The only adjustment he had to make was to learn the pitchers and make a slight adjustment [from an aluminum bat to] a wooden bat. With his makeup and work ethic, I felt he'd adapt very quickly."

But on draft day in 1989, not everyone on the White Sox staff was convinced. They had each seen Thomas play and read Rizzo's glowing reports. But the Major League Scouting Bureau listed him as the 81st best prospect. The White Sox, who had the seventh pick, wanted to improve their pitching and were interested in a high school hurler, right-hander Jeff Juden. A heated discussion ensued in the draft room. "I guess I yelled louder than anybody else," Rizzo said.

The draft began and Baltimore selected pitcher Ben McDonald first. Other teams chose a pitcher, catcher and outfielders before it was Chicago's turn. It was decision time and Juden was still available. But Al Goldis had a knack for judging talent. He had chosen pitcher Jack

McDowell in 1987 and third baseman Robin Ventura in 1988. "Al's a hitting guy," Rizzo said, "and he was the guy who pulled the trigger. It's hard to believe now, but that year when they announced Frank Thomas to the White Sox a couple people went, 'Jeez, how could they pick him?'"

"I was hoping Chicago got me," Thomas said.

He wanted to skip the rookie league and open at Class AA. After all, he said confidently, he had enough experience and the Sox needed a first baseman. Carlos Martinez and Greg Walker were the starters for the big league team in 1989 but neither was faring well that year. Thomas wanted to step in immediately.

Rizzo was in Sarasota, Florida, when Thomas signed his first pro contract. He had fought hard for the big first baseman. He knew the White Sox had made the right decision.

# 4

# MAKING THE BIG LEAGUES

"There's some thunder in that lineup now."
— White Sox manager Jeff Torborg

On the first weekend of July 1989, the Chicago White Sox were playing host to the Kansas City Royals and two-sport star Bo Jackson at old Comiskey Park. The White Sox invited Frank Thomas to take some swings in batting practice with the big leaguers. Manager Jeff Torborg could not believe how big this seemingly shy first baseman was. "Dave LaRoche was pitching," Torborg said, "and Frank hit a couple balls that sounded like he broke his bat and he hit them onto the upper deck and I thought 'Wow.'"

Frank Thomas made a good first impression. He split time in 1989 between the White Sox's rookie team in the Gulf Coast League and the Class A Sarasota team. The following spring, he was invited to the big league camp and Torborg did his best to make Thomas feel comfortable. "I wanted him to feel more at home," Torborg said. "I didn't want him to feel like the manager was a distant guy. We'd just talk at times, casual talks, like father and son things." Torborg, who had three sons of his own, could easily switch from father figure to manager. And he could sense Frank Thomas was a special player. Thomas did everything to

*Thomas's hitting was good enough for him to make the major leagues in 1990, but he was awkward in the field and had an erratic arm. The White Sox sent him down to the AA Birmingham Barons for more experience.*

impress the big league team, hitting two heart-stopping home runs in seven exhibition games. One of them, off a full-count breaking ball from Texas pitcher Nolan Ryan, cleared the left field scoreboard at the Texas Rangers' Port Charlotte, Florida, stadium. "I didn't measure it," Torborg said, "but it was a blast. It looked like 500 feet."

White Sox general manager Larry Himes did not want to rush Thomas, but Torborg liked the first baseman more and more with each swing that spring. "I said to Larry, 'Are you sure we can't have this guy?'" Torborg said. "Larry said he wasn't sure Frank was ready defensively."

The problem was Thomas's erratic throwing. He had an awkward short-arm motion from the side. He threw one ball into the dirt in front of home plate trying to snare a runner, and another time sailed a ball over the dugout. Because the White Sox were in the American League, Torborg felt he could hide Thomas's defensive lapses by using him as the designated hitter and giving him time to develop.

"Our lineup looks a lot better with him in it," Torborg said to Himes, and constantly fought for the big, quiet kid from Georgia. Himes decided to wait. The White Sox knew Thomas could swing the bat, knew he was a talented prospect, but they also knew he needed some experience at a higher level in the minor leagues. He was assigned to Class AA Birmingham, where coach Doug Mansolino, then the defensive coordinator for the minor leagues, caught up with him. It was Mansolino's job to help players improve their defensive abilities. The first time he saw Thomas in a game, the first baseman tripped over the bag while trying to field a ground ball. "'Manso,' you've got a lot of work to do," said Jim Snyder, the minor league field director in

*White Sox Manager Jeff Torborg had two former Auburn football players on the 1991 team: Bo Jackson, seen here on the left with Torborg, and Thomas. A Heisman trophy winner in 1985, Jackson was an All-Star outfielder until a hip injury cut short his career.*

1990 for the White Sox. Mansolino said: "I know, I know."

The two started a work regimen that continued throughout Thomas's major league career. Mansolino would hit ground ball after ground ball to Thomas. After one game in Birmingham, Thomas was headed off the field to take a friend to dinner. Mansolino stopped him. "Frank, we've got work to do," the coach said, and they practiced for two more hours.

Hitting was no problem. Thomas batted .323 for the Barons with 18 home runs in big Hoover Metropolitan Stadium in suburban Birmingham, the toughest ballpark to hit in in the Southern League. It was 405 feet to dead center at the Hoover Met and a batter really had to crush a ball to clear the eight-foot fence.

In Chicago, Thomas's minor league exploits were becoming legendary. "It got to the point where nobody ever used his last name," said Danny Evans, director of baseball administration for the Sox. "Every morning, our people would ask, 'What did Frank do last night?'" At the end of July, the White Sox were in Boston for a three-game series. They were in a mini-slump, three games back in the American League West. Torborg, who talked to Himes daily, knew the White Sox needed some pop in the lineup. "We've got to do something," Torborg said to Himes, who responded, "How would you like to have Frank Thomas and [pitcher] Alex Fernandez?"

Torborg didn't hesitate. "Yes sir—please, please, please, please," he said.

"I was shocked," Thomas said, remembering the day he was called up. "They said, 'Clean out your locker. You're going to [join the White Sox in] Milwaukee.'"

Alex Fernandez had been the White Sox' top draft pick in June and had a 3–0 record in four games for Birmingham. The two joined the major league team at Milwaukee County Stadium on August 2 and never looked back. In his first big league start, Thomas drove in the game-winning run on an 85-foot grounder, his first career RBI, in the eighth inning of a 4–3 win over the Brewers. The next night, August 3, Thomas hit a two-run triple off the top of the right field fence at County Stadium in the White Sox' 6–2 win over Milwaukee. The extra-base hit in the eighth inning off Milwaukee pitcher Mark Knudson ricocheted off the top of the 10-foot wall about 325 feet from the plate, then rolled away from outfielder Rob Deer who collided with the fence.

Thomas still showed some rough edges. He committed his first big league error before he got his first hit when he took a Dave Parker bouncer on the chest in the fourth inning of the August 3 game. Torborg pulled Thomas for a defensive replacement in his first three games. "I've got to get myself calmed down," Thomas said. "I'm still excited."

So were the White Sox. "There's some thunder in that lineup now," Torborg said.

*It's like facing an onrushing freight train when Frank Thomas roars down the basepath intent on breaking up a double play. Yankees second baseman Pat Kelly leaps for his life and fails to turn the twin killing.*

Thomas showed a remarkable eye for a 22-year-old kid. He struck out only once in his first 28 major league plate appearances. Between Birmingham and Chicago, he drew 156 walks, the most in all baseball. A 13-game hitting streak in September helped him earn American League Player of the Week honors. He finished with a .330 batting average, seven home runs and 11 doubles, erasing all doubts that he was ready for the major leagues. "I deserve to be here," he said.

Great hitters have the ability to concentrate on a different level from ordinary players. They can zone in on a pitcher, block out all distractions and produce. Torborg saw that instantly with Thomas. Rather than try to pull pitches, Thomas would wait and use the entire field. He did not hit his first home run for a while but Torborg wasn't worried. He was hitting the ball hard all over the ballpark. "From the first day, he never seemed intimidated by great pitchers, situations or anything," Torborg said. "It was almost like he should've hit anyone. It was nothing brash. He's just very confident."

Thomas always appeared to know exactly what he wanted to do at the plate. Sometimes he would chase a bad pitch, but then he would step away from the plate, take a deep breath, regroup and come through with a base hit. "He was such a good off-speed hitter," Torborg said. "The first thing people do when they see a young hitter is that you think he can't hit the breaking ball. Boy, were they wrong. All the great hitters—like Willie Mays—were great off-speed hitters. You don't make a mistake with Frank with a breaking ball. He'll make you pay."

# 5

# TROUBLES WITH
# THE GLOVE

"I've got a lot to prove."
— Frank Thomas

Dave Parker and Dave Winfield were Frank Thomas's role models, mainly because they also were big ballplayers. "I wanted to be like them—big and intimidating," Thomas said. But being powerful also had its drawbacks. "People have high expectations. They're looking for me to be a 40 home run man." His goal remained to bat .300 and let the other things like the home runs and the RBI take care of themselves.

Thomas struggled at the start of the 1991 season. Heading into a game against Baltimore on April 22, he was batting a disappointing .200. White Sox manager Jeff Torborg had dropped Thomas to sixth in the batting order from the cleanup spot the previous game, hoping to take some pressure off the big first baseman.

This was the White Sox' first season in the new Comiskey Park, built across the street from the old ballpark. One of the old stadium's trademarks was the exploding scoreboard that would shoot fireworks into the sky whenever a Sox player homered. On April 22, the first night game at new Comiskey, Thomas ignited the pyrotechnics for the first time in the fifth inning against the

*When 5-foot-8 second baseman Joey Cora and 250-pound Frank Thomas go after the same pop fly, Cora is wise to fall out of harm's way to avoid a collision.*

Orioles' Ben McDonald. His two-run homer into the seats in left center field opened a 6–5 lead en route to an 8–7 victory. "I went up there with a different attitude," said Thomas, who refused a curtain call despite the cheers from the 30,480 fans at the new park. "I wanted to get something accomplished."

The home run also seemed to ignite him. He batted .412 in his next nine games, and finished his first full season in the majors with a .318 average, 32 homers and 109 RBI. He was third in the voting for Most Valuable Player behind Cal Ripken Jr. and Cecil Fielder, an impressive beginning. But he also had to play 101 games as the designated hitter because of his rawness at first base and a slight shoulder injury. Following the 1991 season, orthopedic surgeon Dr. Frank Jobe performed arthroscopic surgery on Thomas's right shoulder, removing the scar tissue that had developed from all the weight lifting he had done in college. "His arm was killing him," Torborg said. "Part of the reason was that we were all trying to help him [with his throwing]. One person said 'You should throw over the top' and another person had a different way. Everybody wanted to help him. We just knew he was struggling. Every day I asked him how he was feeling and I said, 'When you're ready to play first base, let me know.' To his credit, even with a sore arm, I knew he wanted to. He wanted to be a complete player."

Because of the operation that October, Thomas had to recuperate slowly and could not lift weights or train as hard as usual during the off season. The White Sox were not discouraged. As long as he could hit, they wanted him in the lineup. In March 1992, Thomas signed a three-year contract that would pay him $5 million if he achieved all of the incentives, which included $100,000 if he was named Most Valuable Player. "It shows the confidence we have in Frank," White Sox owner Jerry Reinsdorf said. Earlier that spring, the Sox also signed third baseman Robin Ventura to a two-year, $2.3 million deal. The cornerstones of the White Sox were set.

The expectations were high for Thomas. "I've learned this much," he said prior to his second full big league season in 1992, "a player can't take anything for granted. I have a gift. But that means I have to work extra hard to get better. Concentration is the key. I try not to be distracted." He was not a typical right-handed power hitter. Only 12 of his 32 home runs in 1991 were hit to left field. But even more remarkable was that Thomas drew 138 walks in his first full season, the youngest player to walk that many times since Ted Williams in 1941. "I can't force the action," Thomas said. "The percentages are against you when you're swinging at balls outside the strike zone. If it's not a strike, I don't swing." Thomas's gift was his eye and his ability to wait for the pitch he wanted.

Even though he did well offensively in 1992, he continued to struggle at first base. Because of the surgery, he could not take as many grounders at first as he normally did, so he did not get much practice. It showed. "I made a couple errors and I lost confidence over there," Thomas said. "I shouldn't do that." He finished with 13 errors in 158 games at first, second highest among American League first basemen.

It was an eventful year for Thomas, who had gotten married in the off-season to Elise Silver

*Beginning in Birmingham, White Sox coach Doug Mansolino's job was to make a first baseman out of Frank Thomas. Hitting ground balls for hours at a time both before and after games, Mansolino continued to work with Thomas on his fielding and throwing in Chicago. "He takes a lot of pride in his work," Mansolino said.*

and celebrated the birth of their first child, son Sterling, on July 14, 1992, at the All-Star break. Thomas led the American League in extra-base hits and on-base percentage and batted .323 with 24 homers and 115 RBI, but he was a disappointing eighth in the controversial Most Valuable Player balloting. Oakland closer Dennis Eckersley won the award, normally presented to a position player, not a pitcher. Finishing so low in the MVP voting angered Thomas because he felt few players in baseball had a better offensive year. As for his defensive weakness, "That can be an excuse for me not winning, that's all it can be," Thomas said. "MVP's an offensive award. Offense sells tickets and that's the way it's been for years and that's been winning the MVP for years." Eckersley had saved 51 games that year for the Athletics and also won the Cy Young Award, presented to the top pitcher in the league. "The MVP is not a pitcher's award," Thomas said.

Losing the MVP award seemed to inspire Thomas. He dedicated himself after the 1992 season to an intensive winter of weight training. "I know what I can do when I'm strong," he said. Thomas also wanted to change the image that he was a liability at first base. He told coach Doug Mansolino to expect him early in spring training camp in 1993. "We're going to work," Thomas said.

That February and March, the two went through bags and bags of balls, fine-tuning the big first baseman so that he was prepared for anything. "If we had to be on the field for work at nine o'clock, he'd be there at quarter of eight ready to go," Mansolino said. "We did all kinds of stuff—balls in the dirt, ground balls, balls out of machines, pop ups. We dealt with any type of situation that could arise, anything you can think of: fielding bunts, throws to first, throws to third, whatever it may have been." And if they could not fit their practice time in before the team's regular morning workout, Thomas and Mansolino would meet at the end of the day on a half field next to the White Sox' training facility in Sarasota, Florida.

Sometimes Mansolino would round up a few hitters and flip them some balls so Thomas could see the rotation and top spin on the ball, helping to develop better reaction time. That was Thomas's favorite drill and would lock him in. Mansolino believed Thomas could win a Gold Glove, the top defensive award presented to a player in each league at each position. "He takes a lot of pride in his work," Mansolino said.

# 6

# IMAGE IS EVERYTHING

"Playing with Frank is like being part of history."

— Julio Franco

**A**ll of the extra ground balls he took and the effort he put into becoming a complete player paid off for Frank Thomas in 1993 when he won the Most Valuable Player award, only the eighth player to be unanimously chosen. "This is the first season I put everything together," he said. The trophy capped a successful year for the White Sox, who finished first in the American League West division under manager Gene Lamont. Pitcher Jack McDowell won the Cy Young award, Lamont was named Manager of the Year, and pitcher Jason Bere finished second in the Rookie of the Year balloting. However, the White Sox lost, four games to two, to Toronto in the best-of-seven American League Championship Series.

All of baseball was in awe of Thomas. "After he played a couple years and gained the confidence that it takes to perform at this level, you could see that he was going to be a terror because he's got that great eye," said Cecil Fielder, another big ballplayer who knows a thing or two about what it takes to hit major league home runs. "He also made pitchers realize that he wasn't going to swing

*A disciplined hitter who knows the strike zone, Thomas will take a base on balls rather than swing at bad pitches. Sometimes a brave pitcher will brush him back off the plate. The zebra shoes he wears were designed for his "Big Hurt" label.*

at bad pitches, so they had to come at him and try to get him out. That's what helps him tremendously; they know he's not going to swing at bad pitches. When he gets people in scoring position, the pitcher thinks, 'Okay, if I walk him, I might give up one run. If I don't walk him, I might give up four.'"

More often than not, Thomas did draw a walk, and was criticized for not being more aggressive at the plate. Jeff Torborg, who was Thomas's first major league manager, said he was just as satisfied with the free pass. "I kept telling Frank, 'This is your game. Don't you come out of it just because it looks like we need more runs,'" Torborg said. "When guys start chasing bad balls—just the stats alone will tell you—they get in trouble, but Frank has a unique ability to focus on hitting and be selective. That's special."

Thomas headed into the 1994 season determined to show baseball that winning the MVP was no fluke. The White Sox had added some pop in the lineup in designated hitter Julio Franco, who had spent the last five seasons in Texas. He was just what Thomas needed.

In May, Thomas batted an astounding .452 and rekindled talk of possibly becoming the first Triple Crown winner since Carl Yastrzemski in 1967. "I don't think anybody can do it anymore," Lamont said of winning the home run, RBI and batting average title in the same year, "but if anybody can, it's [Frank]."

San Diego's Tony Gwynn, an extraordinary hitter himself who had won six National League batting titles, confessed to tuning his satellite dish to White Sox games so he could keep up to date on Thomas's exploits. "He's fun to watch for me because he does a lot of things that, if you read the hitting books, they tell you not to do," Gwynn said. "His back foot comes off the ground, his top hand comes off the bat—and he still does amazing things."

On July 7, Thomas went 4-for-4 with two doubles and one RBI in a 9-5 White Sox win over Detroit. At that point in the season, Thomas was batting .413 over his last 45 games. "I think the batting race is helping me concentrate more," he said. "I'm trying to hit the ball hard, not go deep. I'm concentrating on getting the barrel of the bat on the ball. I like this feeling." During the series in Detroit, Thomas hit a home run off Tiger pitcher Joe Boever that nearly hit the roof in left field at Tiger Stadium. When Thomas returned to his position at first base, there was a message scrawled in the ground near the bag.

"Wow," wrote Tiger first baseman Mickey Tettleton.

Thomas scrawled his thanks in the dirt.

Just two days after his four-hit game in Detroit, Thomas drove in five runs in an 11–7 White Sox victory over the Milwaukee Brewers. "It's a Catch-22," Milwaukee manager Phil Garner said of Chicago's lineup. "You [walk Thomas] and you start all over with Franco. That's what happens when you get a couple of guys backing each other up like that."

Franco batted fourth behind Thomas in every game but one that season and had the best view of the White Sox' franchise player.

"Playing with Frank," Franco said, "is like being part of history."

At the All-Star Game in Pittsburgh, Thomas stole the show in the home run hitting contest, launching a 519-foot blast off the upper deck at

*Thomas punishes Toronto catcher Pat Borders in a collision at home plate, scoring from first on a double by George Bell. Thomas is the only player in major league history to bat .300 or better with at least 20 home runs, 100 runs batted in, 100 walks and 100 runs scored in six consecutive years.*

Three Rivers Stadium that drew gasps and a standing ovation. But Seattle's Ken Griffey Jr. got salaams when he hit seven home runs, including five into the top deck.

"This is Thomas's fourth year in the league and we still don't know how to pitch to him. Nobody does," Toronto manager Cito Gaston said. "The only time he doesn't do well is when he's swinging at bad pitches and he doesn't do that—not very often."

"Frank Thomas is more than a home run hitter," said Joe Black, a former pitching star with the Brooklyn Dodgers. "A power hitter who hits .380 comes along once in a generation. He's

like Mickey Mantle, except Mantle was quicker. I used to love watching Mantle in batting practice to see how far he hit the ball. Until I saw 'The Hurt,' Mantle was the strongest hitter I had seen."

Thomas also discovered that being at the top of his game did not shield him from criticism. On July 23, at Cleveland's new Jacobs Field, the White Sox were trailing the Indians. In the third inning, Thomas tried to score from second base on a single by Robin Ventura. But Indians catcher Sandy Alomar Jr. had the ball and was blocking home plate. Thomas realized well after he had rounded third base that he was in trouble and hesitated as he came running down the line. Alomar easily tagged him out. "Maybe he took it easy on me," Alomar said, relieved that Thomas did not hit him full force. "I could've been the 'Big Crushed.'"

Some of the media chastised Thomas for being too easy on Alomar. The problem stemmed from a TV commercial Thomas did for Reebok, which had come out with a "Big Hurt" cross-training shoe. In the advertisement, Thomas barreled around third base and crashed into the catcher like a big train with no second thoughts about anyone's safety. In real life, Thomas had jumped off the track rather than risk a collision.

He bristled at the criticism. "What does the world want me to do? Hurt someone?" Thomas said. "That's not my image. I don't want it to be my image."

When he first arrived in the big leagues, Thomas had taped a hand-written reminder on his locker: "DBTH." It stood for "Don't believe the hype," a subtle message to help him stay level headed despite all the accolades he might receive. Thomas thought he had kept his ego in check and that he had handled superstardom well. He knew the importance of image, and his good looks and skills had made him a hot property. There was a Frank Thomas video game, Frank Thomas shoes, and Frank Thomas sunglasses. But there also were Frank Thomas critics. He would learn to deal with them.

The White Sox were in first place in the new American League Central Division in August 1994, but everything came to a crashing halt on August 12 when the major league ballplayers went on strike. Instead of being in the playoffs, Thomas was home with his family—wife Elise, two-year-old son Sterling and daughter Sloan, born March 23. "I didn't get enough baseball out of me," he said.

Life in the Thomas household changed. The emphasis shifted to plans for a new house being

*Thomas's two-year-old son, Sterling, watches as his dad answers reporters' questions on October 26, 1994 after being named the American League's Most Valuable Player for the second year in a row.*

built southwest of Chicago instead of preparing for that night's opponent. "It's a lot different for me to look at Frank on the ballfield as opposed to being in the house," Elise said. "It's almost like he's two separate people. He's not a super-star at home."

Despite the labor problems, postseason honors were awarded and Thomas won his second Most Valuable Player award, finishing the shortened season with a .353 average and 38 home runs. He was the first back-to-back American League winner since Roger Maris in 1960 and 1961. "I'm really disappointed we're not in the World Series," Thomas said. "But this [MVP] is something I can smile about."

# 7

# THE BIG BLURT

"I said some things I shouldn't have said."
— Frank Thomas

*Thomas talks hitting with Ken Griffey Jr. of the Seattle Mariners, his closest rival for American League home run honors. Both sluggers had a chance to set records before a players' strike cost them six weeks of the 1994 season.*

Some ballplayers played golf during the strike of 1994. Many spent quality time with their families, home for the first time in years during August and September. Frank Thomas took advantage of the free time to further develop his business, "Big Hurt Enterprises," which he had established in the spring of 1993. He opened an office in downtown Chicago on the 35th floor of the John Hancock building on Michigan Avenue. He spent days signing zillions of baseballs to fulfill contractual obligations or modeling for a Chicago men's clothing store. Reebok designed a cross-training shoe specifically for Thomas and he had final approval on the colorful suggestions. Any shoe would be hard to miss on Frank's size 13 feet, but Reebok wanted to make certain they were noticed. The shoe company had to use the White Sox silver and black colors, and chose a black and white zebra-striped design. On the back heel of the shoe was Thomas' new "Big Hurt" logo.

Thomas applied his newfound star status to a good cause, donating $50,000 every year to the Leukemia Society of America in memory of his younger sister Pamela, who had died of the disease when he was 10 years old.

He established a charity golf event and planned a ticket program for Chicago-area underprivileged kids to be implemented once baseball resumed. "I guess what people don't know about him," said White Sox broadcaster and former big league pitcher Ed Farmer, "is that his heart is the size of his body."

Despite baseball's unpopular strike, Thomas received hundreds of requests for personal appearances or autographs. He even appeared on David Letterman's late night television show and swung a bat at a tomato, a grapefruit and a canteloupe off a batting tee. "That's the first swing since the strike began," Thomas said.

Thomas had planned to expand his business interests once his baseball career was over. Even though he got a head start because of the extra time off, he would have preferred driving to Comiskey Park rather than his downtown Chicago office. His thoughts kept returning to baseball. "I'm not putting any limitations on what I can do now," he said. "Mentally, I've got a mind set that 'Hey, I should hit 50 home runs and drive in 130 runs with a .350 batting average.' That was something I always felt I could do, but this was the first season I really put it all together."

One of the reasons Thomas had so much success in his second MVP season was the presence of Julio Franco in the White Sox line-up, creating a powerful one-two punch. Thomas signed a new four-year, $29 million contract prior to the 1995 season with option years at $7 million each for 1999 and 2000. However, White Sox general manager Ron Schueler was unable to meet Franco's salary request for the 1995 season, so Franco decided instead to play in Japan. Thomas issued a statement criticizing management for not doing everything it could to keep Franco. "I spoke my mind," Thomas said. "I knew how much that hitter meant behind me in the lineup." Instead of Franco, former Cincinnati third baseman Chris Sabo was the designated hitter when the White Sox opened the strike-delayed 1995 season on April 26.

Baseball desperately needed to win back its fans after the long, tense layoff. The White Sox tried to entice people to go early to the ballpark by switching the batting practice schedule at Comiskey Park so the visiting team would hit first, then the Sox. That way, when the gates opened two hours before game time, fans could watch their team hit. But baseball players are creatures of habit and Thomas was upset because the change disrupted his pregame schedule. Some ballplayers' routines border on being superstitious. Third baseman Wade Boggs would eat chicken before every game. Relief pitcher Turk Wendell ate black licorice during a game and brushed his teeth between innings. Pitcher David Wells listened only to heavy metal music the day he started.

The White Sox season started on a bad note. On Opening Day, Milwaukee's John Jaha hit a grand slam off Chicago starter Alex Fernandez in the first inning and the Brewers won 12–3.

In five April games, the White Sox committed 19 errors. Thomas hit safely in all five of those games, including a pair of home runs. But Sabo struggled early at the plate, the mistakes mounted and the pitching faltered. The White Sox fell to fourth place in the American League Central

Division at the end of May. Thomas tried to pick up the slack by himself.

"I think when guys hit good around Frank, obviously, that's when he's going to be better," teammate Robin Ventura said. "Sometimes he might not hit as well because people aren't going to pitch to him, so he kind of chases bad pitches. I think he tries to do more—not that he's not capable of doing that—but he tries to do more than what's given to him."

Thomas could only do so much. The White Sox fell 10 games behind Cleveland in the division by June 1 and manager Gene Lamont was fired. In new manager Terry Bevington's debut on June 2, Thomas hit the 35th first-inning home run of his career, but it was Ozzie Guillen's run-scoring double in the 15th inning that gave Chicago a 5–4 victory over Detroit.

Thomas found himself putting his foot in his mouth at the All-Star break in July. Rather than play in the game, he said he would not mind taking the three days off to rest. Unfortunately,

*When the 1994 season ended on August 12, Thomas turned his attention to his "Big Hurt Enterprises" business interests. Here he poses for an ad for a Chicago clothing store.*

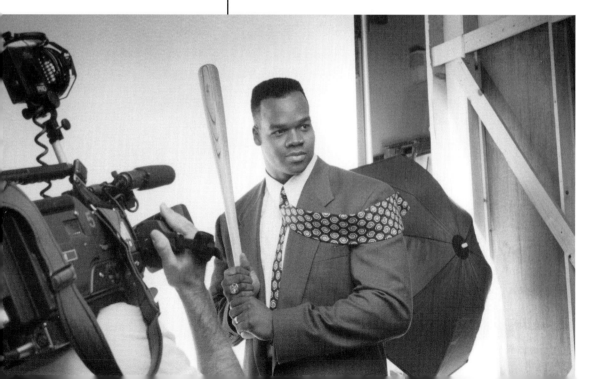

he sounded selfish and unappreciative of the fans who vote for the All-Stars. "I said some things I shouldn't have said," he admitted. He did go to Texas for the All-Star Game and won the home run hitting contest on the first day of the festivities. He started at first base for the American League in the game and hit a two-run home run but left before the contest ended so he could catch a flight home. The White Sox were holding a workout the day after the All-Star Game and Thomas wanted to be with his teammates in Chicago. Again, the media criticized him, saying Thomas was thinking only of himself by not being available to reporters after the game.

"Frank did the right thing," Bevington said in Thomas's defense. "There were much more important things at hand than for Frank Thomas to be sitting on the bench and cheering."

Thomas could not understand why he was being so harshly criticized, especially by the White Sox fans. One Chicago newspaper columnist called him "The Big Blurt."

"I try not to listen to that stuff," Thomas said of the criticism. "I try to play the same everywhere. I give it all I've got every time, whether it's at home or on the road, but it's weird how some things turn around."

Being in the limelight had its disadvantages. Not only was Thomas supposed to be perfect at baseball, but also in everything he did. He thought it was unfair to be judged differently than most people. And every time he said something, it became front page news. "I'm trying to make sure I say the right thing," said Thomas, who became very cautious around reporters' microphones and notebooks. "Sometimes you say things and you don't realize how they will be interpreted by the media."

Thomas also sought advice from his boss, White Sox owner Jerry Reinsdorf, who had been blamed for the players' strike. "I told him I was getting bashed for no reason," Thomas said. "I felt bad because everything seemed to be turning fans against me. He [Reinsdorf] said, 'That's going to happen. They're going to tear you down if they can. Be careful what you say.'"

The distractions did not affect his performance on the field. He became the first player ever to bat .300 with 20 home runs, 100 RBI, 100 walks and 100 runs in five consecutive seasons. Hall of Famers Lou Gehrig and Ted Williams had been the only players to reach those figures in four consecutive seasons. Thomas hit .308 with 40 home runs—he hit the 40th home run on the last day of the season—and had 111 RBI and 136 walks.

And he was only 27 years old.

He could not singlehandedly save the White Sox, who finished 32 games behind the Cleveland Indians with a 68–76 record. "I've never been on a losing team," said Thomas, who lost his bid to win a third MVP award. "It's weird. It's a reality check. This is something definitely different for me." The frustrating season was not something he wanted to repeat.

Before play started in 1996, the White Sox juggled their roster again and added outfielders Danny Tartabull and Darren Lewis and pitcher Kevin Tapani as well as reacquiring designated hitter Harold Baines. Baines, one of the most consistent hitters in baseball, had played for the White Sox for 10 seasons and ranked second all-time on the team with 186 home runs. Thomas was third with 182 homers.

The season started well. Thomas got into a groove early, batting .378 in April with eight home runs and 23 RBI. At the All-Star break, Chicago was only two games behind the Indians in the Central Division. The White Sox won three out of four games against Cleveland prior to the break and had the best pitching staff in the American League. But the series against the Indians was one Thomas would painfully remember. While running around first base in the first game on July 4 he injured his foot—yet stayed in the game and played the entire weekend despite the pain. When Thomas arrived in Philadelphia for the All-Star Game, his foot was so sore and swollen he could not participate in the home run hitting contest or the game the next day. "My concern now is the rest of the season," said Thomas, who was leading the majors with 85 RBI at that time. "I don't know how I played in Cleveland."

It turned out the injury was more serious than anybody thought. Thomas found out he had a stress fracture in his left foot the same day—July 11—that his wife Elise gave birth to their third child, a girl named Sydney Blake. His consecutive game streak was over at 346 and he was told to stay off his feet for three weeks. "I don't like being a cheerleader," he said, "but you can't control injuries." At that point in the season, Thomas ranked among the league leaders with a .349 average and 23 home runs.

The White Sox used Ventura and Dave Martinez at first base in Thomas's absence but the team went 7–11 while he was on the disabled list July 11–29, batting a dismal .253. "Whoever says it's not a big difference without Frank in the lineup is lying to themselves," Sox pitcher

*Frank Thomas fits the mold of two powerful American League right-hand-hitting first basemen who came before him: Jimmie Foxx (top) of the 1920s and 1930s Philadelphia Athletics and Boston Red Sox, and Hank Greenberg of the 1930s and 1940s Detroit Tigers. Foxx, the strongest man in baseball, set the home run record for right-hand batters with 58 in 1932. Greenberg tied the record in 1938.*

Alex Fernandez said. Most important, Chicago had dropped seven games behind Cleveland. The White Sox would never close the gap.

The frustration over losing boiled over in early August at Yankee Stadium. On August 7, Thomas was ejected from the game for arguing a called strike three by home plate umpire Brian O'Nora. The next day, Thomas struck out in the seventh inning against New York's Jeff Nelson and was livid. Mad at himself for being embarrassed by Nelson a second day, Thomas yelled and screamed. Ventura, afraid Thomas would be ejected again, tried to get his teammate to stop his temper tantrum but Thomas, all 6-foot-5, 257 pounds, shoved the smaller Ventura in the chest. Teammates Dave Martinez and Lyle Mouton broke up the fracas in the dugout. "The bottom line," Martinez said, "is we wanted Frank to stay in the game."

The television cameras captured the entire, ugly scene and it was replayed over and over on nearly every station. For three weeks after the incident, Thomas would not talk to the media. He finally explained that he felt the coverage of his outburst was unfair. "My job is to come out and win every day," he said. "I don't want to be a controversial figure."

In September, he focused on hitting. Thomas batted .341 in the final month of the season, hitting an American League-leading 11 home runs. He drove in 24 runs, had a .750 slugging percentage and a .433 on-base percentage to win the league's player of the month award. It was his second such honor for the season—he also won in the first month of play in April.

But the White Sox struggled pitching-wise in the final month of play and finished the year with an 85-77 record, losing a chance at the wild card spot on the second to last day when Baltimore clinched with a victory over Toronto. After trailing by just two games at the break, the White Sox ended 14 1/2 games behind Cleveland in the division.

Again, Thomas was close but fell short of the Triple Crown. He was second in the league with a .349 batting average, ranked eighth with 40 home runs—reaching that figure for the second consecutive year—and was seventh with a career-high 134 RBI. Thomas was only the fourth player in major league history to record 100 or more RBI in each of his first six seasons, joining Al Simmons, Joe DiMaggio and Hal Trosky.

Opposing teams demonstrated all season that they still did not know how to pitch to Thomas. The Boston Red Sox tried to not pitch to him on June 4 when they walked him five times—two of them intentional. They should have considered the same approach on September 15 when Thomas hit three home runs off Red Sox pitchers, the first White Sox player to do so in more than two years.

Minnesota manager Tom Kelly took a different approach. "We're going to pitch to him," Kelly said. "If he beats us, he beats us. We don't like to back off against anybody. Frank is very exciting, very entertaining and as an opposing manager against him, you want to see your people compete against him."

Even though Thomas had another spectacular season, the White Sox were unable to take that next step and reach the playoffs. Thomas's first concern was the team.

"To me, there's not a better offensive player in the game," scout Mike Rizzo said of Thomas.

"Every day, whether he's breaking another Ruth record or a Gehrig record, he's up there with some outstanding players. I knew in my heart of hearts that he was going to be a special ballplayer."

His heart was right.

# CHRONOLOGY

1968    Born Frank Edward Thomas on May 27 in Columbus, Georgia

1986    Signs football scholarship to attend Auburn University but plays
        in only three games his freshman season; joins baseball team

1989    Leads Southeastern Conference with .403 batting average;
        selected by Chicago White Sox in first round (seventh overall)
        of June draft

1990    Starts season at Class AA Birmingham; called up to major league
        team on August 2 and records first major league hit the next
        day, a two-run triple off Milwaukee's Mark Knudson; hits first
        big league home run on August 28 off Minnesota's Gary Wayne

1991    Starts 101 games as designated hitter and 56 at first base in
        first full season with White Sox; marries Elise Silver

1992    Signs three-year, $5 million contract prior to season; bats .343
        in 110 games after moving to third spot in batting order; becomes
        first White Sox player to walk 100 times in consecutive seasons

1993    Wins American League MVP by unanimous vote setting club
        single-season record with 41 home runs and ranking in league
        top 10 in batting average, RBI and walks;

1994    Wins second consecutive MVP award, only 11th player in
        major league history to do so

1995    Signs four-year, $29 million contract through 1998 with
        two option years for $7 million each; drives in 100th run on
        September 13 to become first player in major league history
        to collect 100 walks and 100 RBI in five consecutive years;

1996    Drives in career-high 134 runs and hits 40 home runs despite
        missing one month with broken left foot

# Major League Statistics

## Chicago White Sox

| YEAR | TEAM | G | AB | R | H | 2B | 3B | HR | RBI | AVG | SB |
|---|---|---|---|---|---|---|---|---|---|---|---|
| 1990 | Chi A | 60 | 191 | 39 | 63 | 11 | 3 | 7 | 31 | .330 | 0 |
| 1991 | | 158 | 559 | 104 | 178 | 31 | 2 | 32 | 109 | .318 | 1 |
| 1992 | | 160 | 573 | 108 | 185 | 46 | 2 | 24 | 115 | .323 | 6 |
| 1993 | | 153 | 549 | 106 | 174 | 36 | 0 | 41 | 128 | .317 | 4 |
| 1994 | | 113 | 399 | 106 | 141 | 34 | 1 | 38 | 101 | .353 | 2 |
| 1995 | | 145 | 493 | 102 | 152 | 27 | 0 | 40 | 111 | .308 | 3 |
| 1996 | | 141 | 527 | 110 | 184 | 26 | 0 | 40 | 134 | .349 | 1 |
| **Totals** | | 930 | 3291 | 675 | 1077 | 211 | 8 | 222 | 729 | .327 | 17 |

# FURTHER READING

Cox, Ted. *Frank Thomas: The Big Hurt.* Chicago: Children's Press, 1994.

Inside Pitcher Series. *Chicago White Sox.* New York: Bantam, 1993.

Kramer, Sydelle A. *Baseball's Greatest Hitters.* New York: Random Books for Young Readers, 1995.

Gowdey, David, *Baseball's Super Stars.* New York: Putnam, 1994.

The Sporting News Editors. *Baseball's Hall of Fame: Cooperstown, Where the Legends Live Forever.* Avenal, NJ: Random House Value, 1993.

# INDEX

PICTURE CREDITS

AP/Wide World Photo: pp. 3, 11, 28, 30, 33, 35, 39, 42, 44, 46, 50; Auburn University: p. 20; Cecil Darby: pp. 14, 18, 23, 26; Richard Lasner: p. 8; National Baseball Library and Archive, Cooperstown NY: pp. 54 (bottom), 58; Lois Nicholson collection: p. 54 (top)

CARRIE MUSKAT has covered major league baseball since 1981, beginning with United Press International in Minneapolis. She was UPI's lead writer at the 1991 World Series. A freelance journalist since 1992, she is a regular contributor to *USA Today* and *USA Today Baseball Weekly*. Her work also has appeared in the *Chicago Tribune, Inside Sports* and *ESPN Total Sports* magazine.

JIM MURRAY, veteran sports columnist of the *Los Angeles Times*, is one of America's most acclaimed writers. He has been named "America's Best Sportswriter" by the National Association of Sportscasters and Sportswriters 14 times, was awarded the Red Smith Award, and was twice winner of the National Headliner Award. In addition, he was awarded the J. G. Taylor Spink Award in 1987 for "meritorious contributions to baseball writing." With this award came his 1988 induction into the National Baseball Hall of Fame in Cooperstown, New York. In 1990, Jim Murray was awarded the Pulitzer Prize for Commentary.

EARL WEAVER is the winningest manager in the Baltimore Orioles' history by a wide margin. He compiled 1,480 victories in his 17 years at the helm. After managing eight different minor league teams, he was given the chance to lead the Orioles in 1968. Under his leadership the Orioles finished lower than second place in the American League East only four times in 17 years. One of only 12 managers in big league history to have managed in four or more World Series, Earl was named Manager of the Year in 1979. The popular Weaver had his number, 5, retired in 1982, joining Brooks Robinson, Frank Robinson, and Jim Palmer, whose numbers were retired previously. Earl Weaver continues his association with the professional baseball scene by writing, broadcasting, and coaching.